Dear Sydney,
Be SASSY!
♡POPPY

To my Jimbo, the best bud around

www.mascotbooks.com

Sassy

For more information, please contact:
Mascot Books
560 Herndon Parkway #120
Herndon, VA 20170
info@mascotbooks.com

Library of Congress Control Number: 2017901135

CPSIA Code: PRT0417A
ISBN-13: 978-1-68401-241-1

Printed in the United States

Sassy

by Poppy Hall

He arrived on a Tuesday, 2:30 pm,
looked all around, and cleared his throat phlegm.
"Ahhhhem everyone, my name is Sassy,
I'm new in town, I come from Tallahassee."

As he looked to his left, and he looked to his right,
nobody had heard him, not one single sound bite.
Well, Sassy decided that to make a good friend
his humor and charm he would have to extend.

He trotted around and the first thing he found
was a sneaky barn cat scrunched up on the ground.
"Why helloooo kitty-cat, may I play with you?
My name is Sassy, how do you do?"

The cat was not happy and was clearly annoyed,
"My chances of catching that mouse you destroyed!"
"I'm so sorry," said Sassy, whose feelings were hurt.
"I just wanted a friend," he started to blurt.

The cat, known as Catherine, looked the pig up and down.
After three lengthy seconds she started to frown.

"Look buddy, I'm sorry, you seem nice and all,
but you're as clumsy and loud as a big bowling ball.
I'm a cat, don't you see? I am stealthy and quick.
We cannot be friends when your hooves sound like bricks!"

Poor Sassy was gloomy as he tried to make sense.
He walked away sadly and sat down by the fence.

Then commotion behind him, as he turned 'round to hear.
A gaggle of geese suddenly appeared.
"What's shakin', bacon?" said the head of the bunch.
"You afraid of becoming somebody's lunch?"

This gang, they were bullies, an unhappy cluster—
not proud of themselves, so others they fluster.
As the gang wobbled closer it became plain to see,
they were circling around him, he had nowhere to flee!

Then out of nowhere, with no time to spare,
a pair of big dogs flew through the air!

The geese squawked and squabbled
    and scurried away,
and the dogs woofed like crazy
    as they chased them for play.

When the geese had all cleared, and the dogs had stopped barking,
they looked right at Sassy, and started remarking,
"OH MAN, THAT WAS CRAZY! HOLY COW WAS THAT FUN!
Did you see us? That's not even the fastest we run!"

Not sure what just happened, Sassy stood in a daze,
as he looked at the dogs colored white, black, and greys.

"Hey man, I'm Smuggies and this here is Burly!"
"Thank goodness," said Sassy, "you got here so early!"

The dogs looked at Sassy and said, "Wanna play?
We like to tackle and chase each other all day!"
"Sure!" shouted Sassy. "I've been wanting some mates,"
but they took off before he had the chance to say "wait!"

"Those dogs are too crazy and wild for me,
I guess I am destined to just be lonely."
Sassy slumped away sadly and lay down in the field.
Exhaustion rolled over, to which he would yield.

A shadow engulfed him and he woke up to the sound
of a hoof tapping patiently on the soft ground.
"This is the spot where I take my naps.
Scoot over and give me some room to collapse."

"You're not kicking me out or making mean fun?
Or sprinting away as fast as you can run?"
The horse looked at Sassy confused and unsure,
"Of course not, please stay, I'm not immature."

"Name's Jimbo," he continued to talk with the pig,
"How did you end up here, at these awesome digs?"

As they lay in that grass, surrounded by flowers,
the pair chatted away for many long hours
of the places they'd been and where they were from,
and before Sassy knew it, Jimbo was his best chum.

They began a routine where they'd go on a walk,
then go to their spot and lie down and talk.
"You know," Sassy said, wanting his thoughts off his chest,
"you are my best friend, I feel truly blessed.

No one else really cared or bothered with me,
but you wanted to talk and be friends actually."
Jimbo pondered those words, then he finally spoke,
"Listen up Sassy, what I'm 'bout to say is no joke."

"There are those just like Catherine who like to be alone,
and when they ask you to leave, you cannot be thrown.
There are those like the dogs who have different pursuits.
Recall they included you in their laughs and their hoots?

But then there are fools in a gang full of geese,
stealing happiness and joy from those that they tease.
Never stoop to their level or let them control you,
keep your wits and your head, you'll eventually pull through.

The reason, now Sassy, we get along so well,
is our personalities and interests actually gel.
I'll tell you one last line that I try to live by,
it's made me who I am, and this is why.

Give your best effort and always be kind,
you never know the interesting friends you may find.
So Sassy, look there, do you see someone new?
Now that you've heard what I've said, what do you think we should do?"

On a separate note, several thoughts from the author,
my views on being new, some advice I will offer.
For those just like Sassy in a spanking new place,
don't be scared of the challenges that you may face.

I have been in your shoes and I know it is rough,
but have faith in yourself and believe you are tough.
When one door slams closed, find an open window,
and maybe, no definitely, you will find your Jimbo.

Sassy's Story

This book, oddly enough, was inspired by real life events. When I was a little girl, we used to drive by the same farm every day going to and from school. When I was about six and my brother, Mac, was about three, my mom asked us, "What do you think that pig's name is?" Mac responded, "I think that pig's name is Sassy!" From then on we called him Sassy.

One day we were driving by and all these cars were stopped along the side of the road. We pulled over to find a horse lying down in the field with Sassy sprawled across his back taking a nap. I could not get that image out of my head and decided to create the book around the unlikely friendship between a pig and a horse. I named the horse after my extraordinary grandfather, Jimbo, who has taught me some valuable life lessons about being a good person and a true friend.

About the Author

Poppy Hall grew up in Baltimore, Maryland, and attended Garrison Forest School. She enjoyed playing field hockey and lacrosse as well as painting and drawing. She received her bachelors in Art History and Studio Art from Washington and Lee University. She was an interior designer in New York City for several years until she decided to pursue her love of teaching. Poppy received her masters in Education from The George Washington University, which is where she wrote *Sassy*. *Sassy* won the John Horrworth Book Award. Poppy is now a 5th grade reading teacher at Glebe Elementary in Arlington, Virginia.

A special thank you to Brooke McDonald and Michael Brassert for their generous assistance in creating this book!

Please visit my website for more Sassy news!
www.poppyhall.com